This book belongs to
. . . .

LADYBIRD BOOKS
UK | USA | Canada | Ireland | Australia
India | New Zealand | South Africa

Ladybird Books is part of the Penguin Random House group of companies
whose addresses can be found at global.penguinrandomhouse.com.
ladybird.com

First published 2012. This edition published 2016
003

Printed in China

A CIP catalogue record for this book is available from the British Library

ISBN: 978-0-723-29395-8

Souvenir Storybook

exclusive to

Oink!

I'm Peppa Pig. I hope you enjoy whizzing around on all the fun rides at Peppa Pig World – and jumping up and down in all the muddy puddles!

If you need to find your way around, this book has a brilliant map inside that shows you where everything is. Remember to come and see us all in our house where Mummy Pig is teaching me and George how to make pancakes. I love pancakes – they are yummy!

There are lots of stories and games and puzzles too. You can read them with your mummy or daddy when you get home, to remind you of all the fun you had at Peppa Pig World.

Peppa

Muddy Puddles

Windy Castle

Peppa Pig World

Mr. Potato's Playground

Peppa Pig World

Miss Rabbit's Helicopter Flight

Peppa Pig's Toy Shop

Madame Gazelle's School House

see Peppa and George here!

Peppa's Big Balloon Ride

George's Spaceship Play Zone

Daddy Pig's Big Tummy Cafe

Candy Cat's Games Kiosk

Peppa Pig's House

Grandpa Pig's Little Train

Pedro Pony's Photo Kiosk

Grandpa Pig's Boat Trip

Miss Rabbit's IceCream Parlour

Daddy Pig's Car Ride

George's Dinosaur Adventure

Peppa Pig World

Peppa Pig World ™

Peppa's Balloon Adventure

Peppa and her family are on a balloon ride.
It is Miss Rabbit's first time flying the balloon.
"Higher!" says Peppa.

Oh dear, Teddy has fallen out.
He's stuck in a tree.
"Don't worry," says Daddy Pig.
He uses an anchor to rescue
Teddy. Hooray!

But now the balloon is stuck in a tree.
"Look, we're in Granny and Grandpa Pig's garden," says Peppa.
"Help! We can't get down!"

Grandpa Pig brings a ladder
so everyone can climb down
from the balloon.
"Careful, now," says Granny Pig.
"That was so exciting," says Peppa.

Granny Pig hands out some chocolate cake.
"That was the best balloon ride ever," says Peppa.
"And this is the best chocolate cake ever!"

Dotty Dino

Join the dots to finish this big picture of George's favourite toy.

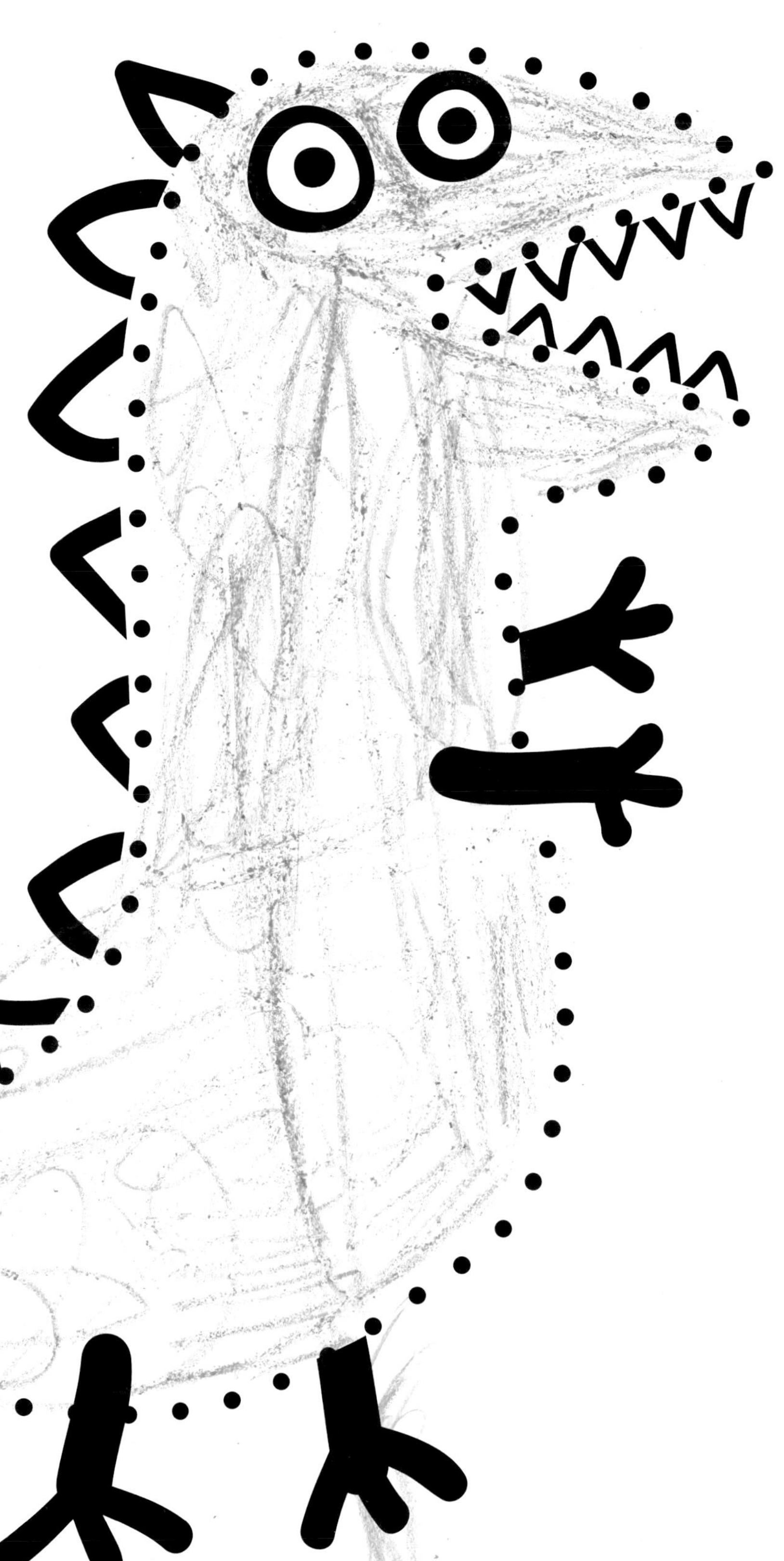

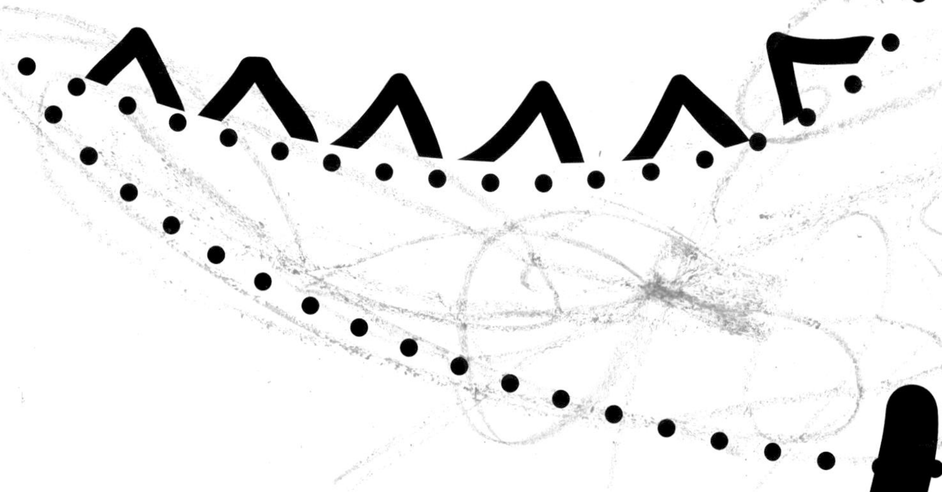

Dine-saw! Grrrr!

Draw lines to match these pictures of George and Mr Dinosaur into pairs. Which one is the odd one out?

Answers: The matching pairs are 'a' and 'g', 'b' and 'f' and 'c' and 'd'. The odd one out is 'e'.

Grandpa's Little Train

Grandpa's little train goes,
Choo, choo, choo!
Choo, choo, choo!
Choo, choo, choo!
Grandpa's little train goes,
Choo, choo, choo!
All day long.

And the piggies on the train go,
Oink, oink, oink!
Oink, oink, oink!
Oink, oink, oink!
And the piggies on the train go,
Oink, oink, oink!
All day long.

All Aboard!

Choo! Choo! Grandpa Pig is taking everyone on a train trip!

How many carriages are there?

How many children are riding in the first carriage?

How many children are riding in the second carriage?

How many wheels are there on the train?

Answers: two; five; five; twelve

Choo! Choo!

Colour this picture of Peppa and George going for a train ride with Grandpa Pig. Use the picture at the top of the page to help you with the colours.

The Boat Pond

Peppa, George, Mummy and Daddy Pig are at the duck pond. The ducks are very happy.

Peppa and George have brought their toy boats to race on the pond. George's boat has to be wound up.

"Click, click, whirrr!"

"Your boat doesn't need winding up, Peppa," says Mummy Pig. "It just needs a little help," says Daddy Pig, blowing Peppa's boat along.

Here is Peppa's friend, Suzy Sheep.
"Hello everyone!" she cries. "I've got my speedboat. It has batteries to make it go!"

Woof! Here is Danny Dog, with Granddad Dog.
"My granddad made me this paddle boat. It's steam powered!" gasps Danny Dog.

Rebecca Rabbit arrives with her mummy.
"I wish I had a boat," she says. "I've got an idea," says Daddy Pig, picking up his newspaper . . .

"When I was a little piggy, I used to fold newspaper to make paper boats!" says Daddy Pig, handing a boat to Rebecca Rabbit.

"Squeak! Thank you, Mr Pig," says Rebecca, placing her paper boat on the pond. "Grunt! Grunt!" George wants a paper boat too!

Daddy Pig makes paper boats for everyone! "Let's race!" says Mummy Pig. "Ready, steady, BLOW!" The boats speed across the pond.

"We have a winner!" says Daddy Pig.
"That's George's boat!" says Peppa.
"George is the winner!"
"Hooray!" everybody cheers.

"I like paper boats the best!" cries Peppa. "Me too!" cry all the children.
It's time to go home. Everybody has had a great day.

"Bye-bye, ducks!"
grunts Peppa. The ducks
enjoyed the toy boats,
but they like having
their pond back too.

Sailing Boats

Peppa and her friends are sailing paper boats on the pond! Can you spot the differences between the two pictures?

I love boats. Snort!

Colour in a sailing boat each time you spot a difference.

Answers:

1. There's a wind-up boat on the pond.
2. Granddad Dog's hat is now pink.
3. Emily Elephant has come to play.
4. One more duck has appeared.
5. Suzy Sheep's dress has changed colour.

Pigs Ahoy!

Chug! Chug! Grandpa Pig is taking everyone on a boat trip! Colour the Pig family in pink, then follow the colour key below to complete the rest of the picture.

Colour key

1 Light blue

2 Pink

3 Purple

4 Dark blue

5 Yellow

6 Brown

Go to www.peppapig.com for more Peppa colouring fun!

1
5
2
6
3
5
4
4

Polly's Boat Trip

Today, Grandpa Pig is taking Peppa and George on a boat trip. Polly Parrot is going too.

"Grandpa Pig! Have you got your mobile telephone?" Granny Pig asks.

"Yes, Granny Pig!" replies Grandpa Pig.

Grandpa Pig starts the engine and the boat begins to sail away.

Peppa, George, Grandpa Pig and Polly Parrot all wave goodbye to Granny Pig.

Sailing down the river, Grandpa Pig sees his best friend, Granddad Dog, cleaning his boat.

"Ho! Ho! I don't know why you bother cleaning that rusty boat! I'm surprised it's still afloat!" jokes Grandpa Pig.

"This rusty boat will still be afloat long after your old tin boat has sunk to the bottom of the river!" laughs Granddad Dog, playfully.

Grandpa Pig, Peppa, George and Polly sail on down the river.
"Now, I am the captain of this boat and when the captain tells you to do something, you must do it," explains Grandpa Pig.
"Aye-aye, Captain!" shout Peppa and George.
Peppa wants to be the captain, so Grandpa Pig gives her his captain's hat. Peppa loves being the captain. Captain Peppa is a bit bossy.

"Perhaps I should be the captain again? We don't want to crash into anything! Snort!" says Grandpa Pig.
Crash! The boat runs aground on to a sand bank.
"Don't worry! I'll ring Granny Pig. She can get help!" says Grandpa Pig.

Polly the Parrot squawks in Grandpa Pig's ear and gives him a fright. "Beep! Beep! Boop! Boop!" she says. Oh dear. Grandpa Pig drops the phone overboard. What are they going to do?
"Snort! I know! Polly can fly to Granny!" says Peppa.
Grandpa Pig teaches Polly what to say to Granny.

Granny Pig is at home and Polly Parrot lands on the telephone.
"Oh! Hello, Polly! What are you doing here?" Granny Pig asks.
"Squawk! Grandpa Pig says Snort! Help! Help!" says Polly.
"Goodness me, Grandpa must need help!" says Granny Pig.

Granny Pig and Polly Parrot jump in the car and drive to the river. They see Granddad Dog on his boat.
"Grandpa Pig needs help! Please could you rescue him?" Granny Pig asks.
"Madame, I would be delighted! Woof!" barks Granddad Dog.

Granddad Dog sails his boat to rescue Grandpa Pig, Peppa and George.
"Would you like my rusty old boat to rescue you?" asks Granddad Dog.
"Aye-aye, Skipper! Snort!" says Grandpa Pig.

Everyone is happy. They all think Polly is a very clever parrot.
"I'm a clever parrot!" says Polly and everyone laughs.

Boat Maze

Grandpa Pig loves to sail his boat. Help him get to shore through this wavy sea maze.

Dot-to-Dot

Can you see what Peppa is eating? Join the dots to find out.

Peppa is eating an ___ ______

Answer: Peppa is eating an ice cream.

What's Missing?

Oh dear! It's raining and Daddy Pig is getting wet! What does he need to stay dry? Use your pencils to finish the picture.

Peppa's Car Ride

It's a lovely sunny day. Peppa and her family are going for a drive. Peppa and George love their red car.

Clank! Boing! Oh dear. The car does not sound very well. They must take it to Granddad Dog's garage.

Granddad Dog lends them a new blue car. It has lots of different buttons. One of the buttons folds the roof down.

Oh dear, it's starting to rain.
Daddy Pig cannot find the button to close the roof and sprays himself with water!
Peppa and George think this is very funny.
Hee! Hee!
Ha! Ha!

Now Granddad Dog has mended their car. The new car was fun, but Peppa likes their old car the best.

Zoom to the Moon

Search this picture of George's space adventure for hidden objects!

Tick the stars when you find these things in the big picture.

How many planets can you see?

Answer: There are four planets.

Up, Up and Away
Peppa and her family are flying high in the sky! Join the dots to find out what they're travelling in.

Granny and Grandpa's Attic

Today, Peppa and George are playing at Granny and Grandpa Pig's house.
"You can help us tidy the attic," says Grandpa.
"What's an attic?" asks Peppa.
"It's where we keep all our old things," replies Grandpa.
"Old like you, Grandpa?" smiles Peppa, cheekily.
"Ha, ha," laughs Grandpa. "Things that are even older than me, Peppa!"

The attic is at the very top of the house.
"Wow!" gasps Peppa. "It's very full!"
"Let's throw this out," says Granny, holding up a bottle.
"That's my ship in a bottle. I need it," replies Grandpa.
"How about this box?"
"No!" cries Granny. "That has my hats inside it."
Oh dear. Granny and Grandpa can't decide what to throw out.

"Let's throw away this old case," suggests Peppa.
"Not that!" shout Granny and Grandpa together!
"That's a record player."
Granny and Grandpa play their favourite music on the record player.
Crackle, crackle.
Peppa, George, Granny and Grandpa dance round and round the room!

"That was so much fun!" smiles Grandpa. "But we are supposed to be finding things to throw out!"
"Hmmm, I think you should just keep . . . everything!" cries Peppa.
"Ha, ha, ha!" everyone laughs.

Grandpa's Garden

Grandpa Pig loves his garden. He grows fruit, vegetables and flowers.

Look at the big picture and count all the items shown opposite. Tick each box when you have counted them all.

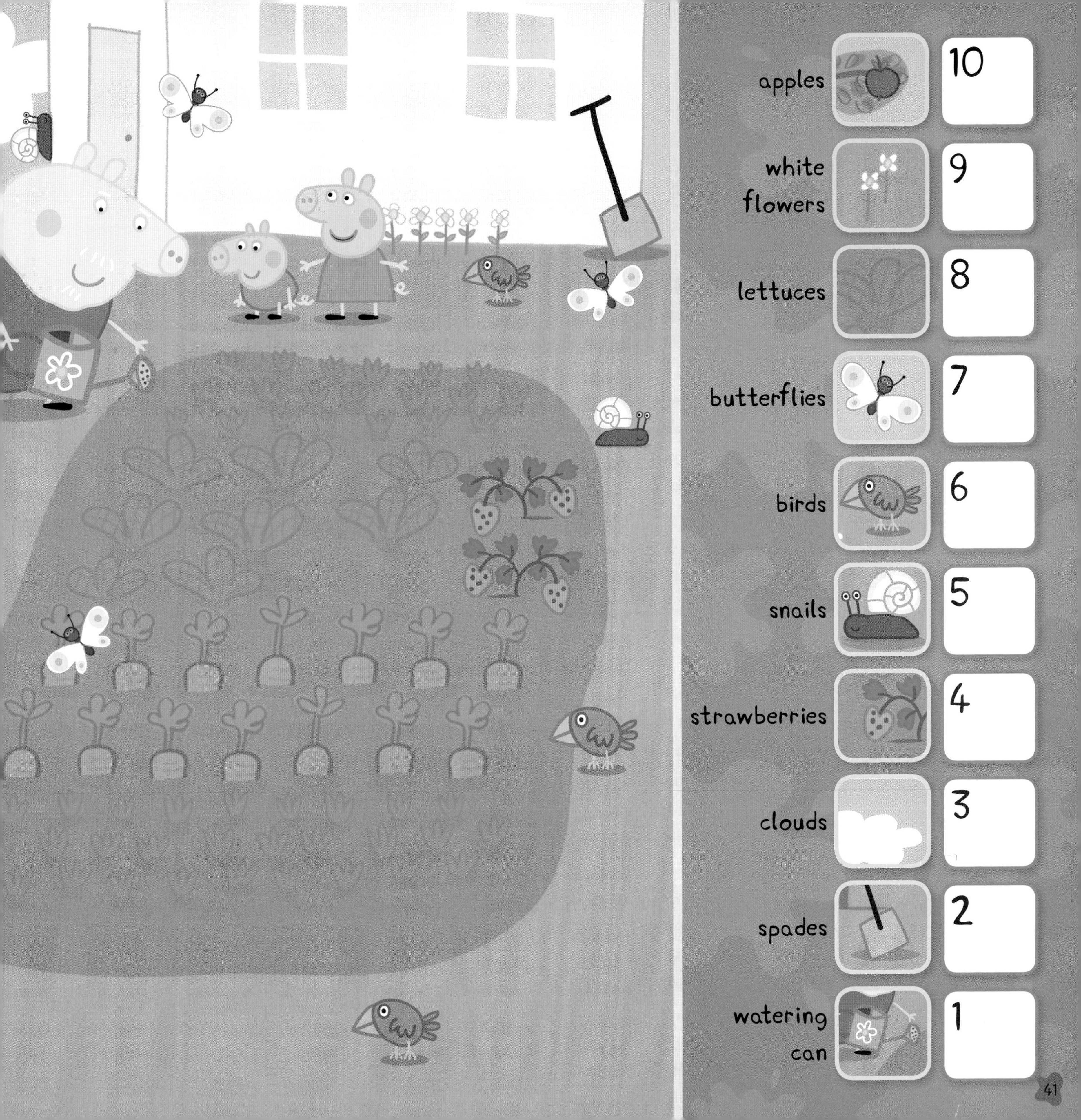
apples
10
white flowers
9
lettuces
8
butterflies
7
birds
6
snails
5
strawberries
4
clouds
3
spades
2
watering can
1

Grandpa's Compost Heap

Everyone is hungry, so Daddy Pig is making vegetable soup for lunch. Yummy!

Peppa helps by clearing away the vegetable peelings. "Good! Granny and Grandpa will like these," says Mummy Pig.

"Do Granny Pig and Grandpa Pig eat banana skins and potato peelings?" asks Peppa. "Ha! Ha! Ha! No, Peppa," says Daddy Pig.

Peppa and George take the peelings to Grandpa Pig.
"Ah! Vegetable peelings! Fantastic! My garden will like these!"
Grandpa Pig says, very pleased.

Grandpa shows Peppa, George and Mummy Pig his compost heap.
"Grunt! It's a wooden box!" smiles Peppa.
"Yes, Peppa, but it's a very clever wooden box," says Grandpa Pig.

Grandpa explains that vegetable peelings go in the top and earth called compost comes out the bottom. Peppa and George look in the box and see wriggly worms amongst the vegetable peelings.

Peppa and George help by digging in the earth, looking for worms.

"Be a good wriggly worm and turn it all into compost!" says Peppa.

Peppa and George add their worms to the peelings.

They all go to find Granny Pig in the orchard.
"Grunt! Hello, everyone!" says Granny Pig.
They shake the tree and apples fall to the ground.
"Hee! Hee! Hee! It's raining apples!" cries Peppa.
Munch! Munch! Munch! Peppa and George eat
their crunchy apples.
They then add their apple cores to the wriggly
worms in the compost heap. Snort! Snort!
"Clever wriggly worms!" says Peppa.

Where's Mr Dinosaur?

Oh no, George has lost his favourite toy!
Can you help him find Mr Dinosaur?

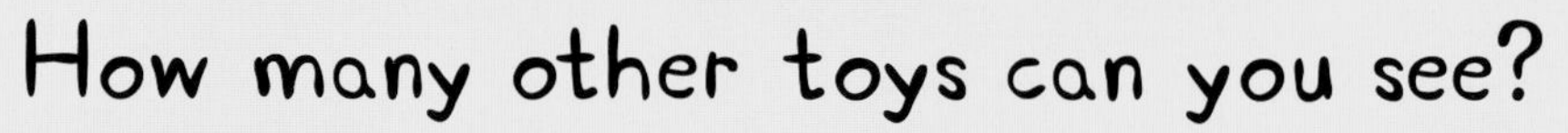

How many other toys can you see?

Answer: six

My Peppa Door Hanger

Ask an adult to help you cut out along the dotted lines. Then fold in half and stick together to make your door hanger.

See you soon!